SCOULAR ANDERSON lives in a house which overlooks the sea.
This means he can spend quite a lot of time looking through his
telescope searching for pirates. So far, he hasn't spotted any so he likes to
write about them instead. He also likes dogs so he writes about them
quite a lot, too. He never writes about horses or bicycles because they have
bits that stick out at odd angles and are very hard to draw.

When he's not writing or illustrating he goes for long walks in the Scottish
mountains to think about new stories. His other book for Frances Lincoln
is *Space Pirates and the Treasure of Salmagundy.*

Space Pirates and the Monster of Malswomp
copyright © Frances Lincoln Limited 2007
Text and illustrations
copyright © Scoular Anderson 2007

The right of Scoular Anderson to be identified
as the author and illustrator of this work has been
asserted by him in accordance with the Copyright,
Designs and Patents Act, 1988.

First published in Great Britain and in the USA
in 2007 by Frances Lincoln Children's Books,
4 Torriano Mews, Torriano Avenue, London NW5 2RZ

www.franceslincoln.com

First paperback edition published in Great Britain
in 2009

British Library Cataloguing in Publication Data
available on request

The illustrations for this book are in watercolour
paints and black pen.

ISBN: 978-1-84507-242-1

Printed in Singapore

9 8 7 6 5 4 3 2 1

Find out more about the adventures of the
Space Pirates on Scoular Anderson's website,
www.scoularanderson.co.uk, or read the first book
in the Space Pirate series, Space Pirates and the
Treasure of Salmagundy.

For Alexander and Orla

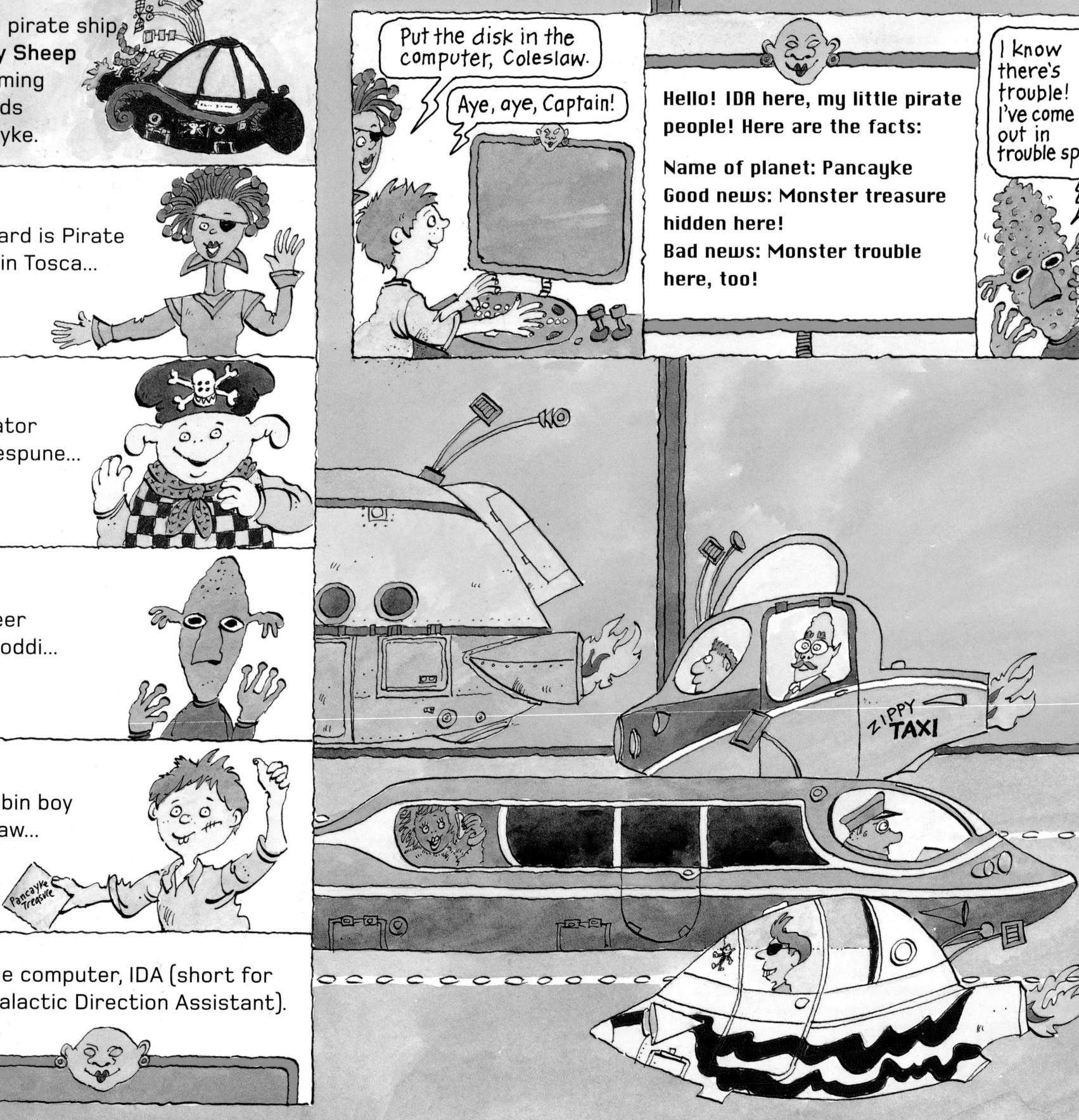

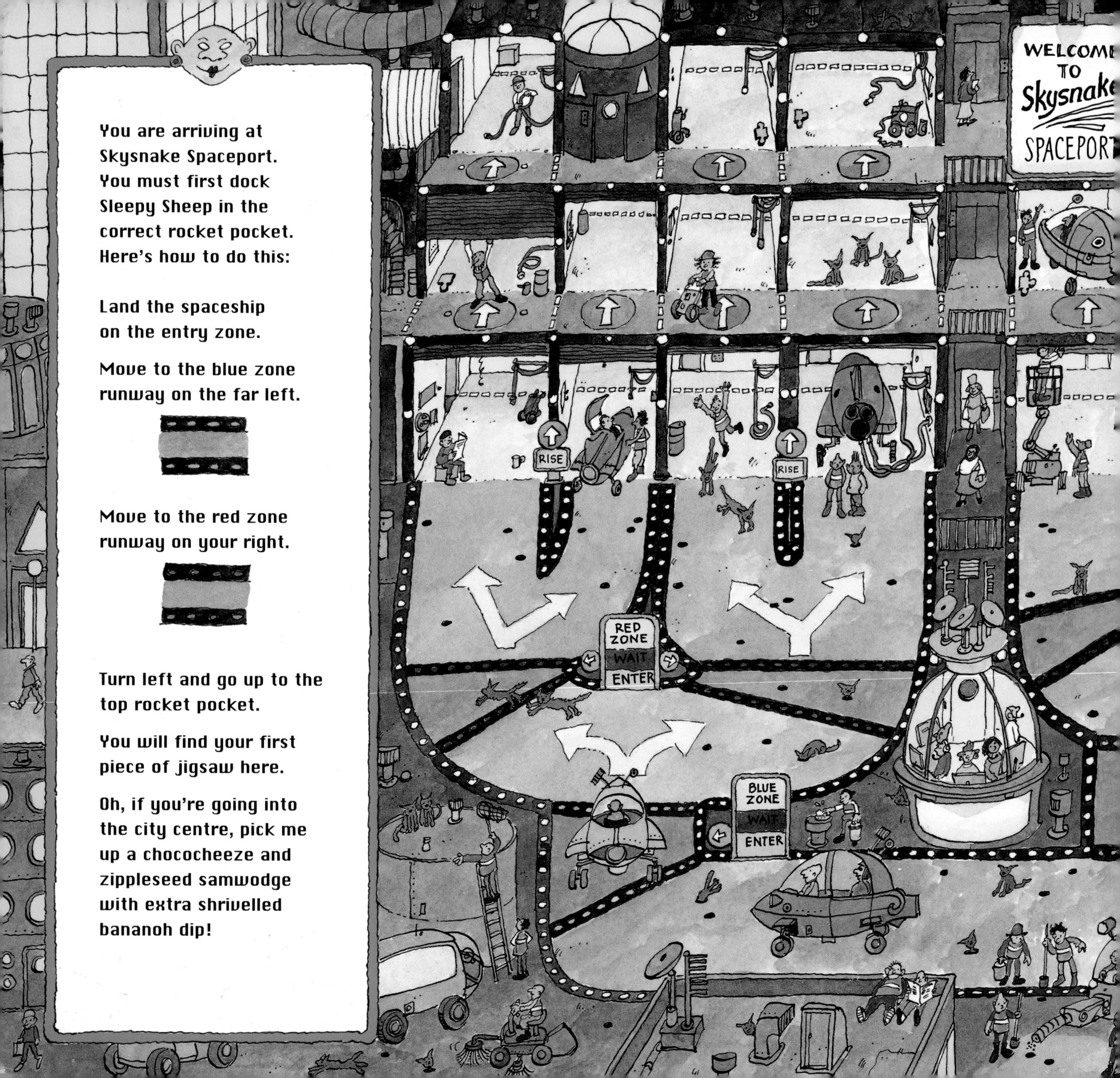

You are arriving at Skysnake Spaceport. You must first dock Sleepy Sheep in the correct rocket pocket. Here's how to do this:

Land the spaceship on the entry zone.

Move to the blue zone runway on the far left.

Move to the red zone runway on your right.

Turn left and go up to the top rocket pocket.

You will find your first piece of jigsaw here.

Oh, if you're going into the city centre, pick me up a chococheeze and zippleseed samwodge with extra shrivelled bananoh dip!

Greetings! IDA here, my brave little beetroots! If you found the right piece of jigsaw at Skysnake Spaceport it should look like this:

Here is a plan of the Sheepshovel Shopping Mall. Use it to find the next jigsaw pieces.

Go into the shopping mall through the front door.

Take the lift from the ground floor to the second floor.

Go up the escalator to the third floor. Find a piece of jigsaw nearby.

Go down the stairs to the first floor. You will find another piece of jigsaw nearby.

Right now. Where shall I start? I'd like a pancake or two with spugfruit jelly and a good dollop of creamble, then...

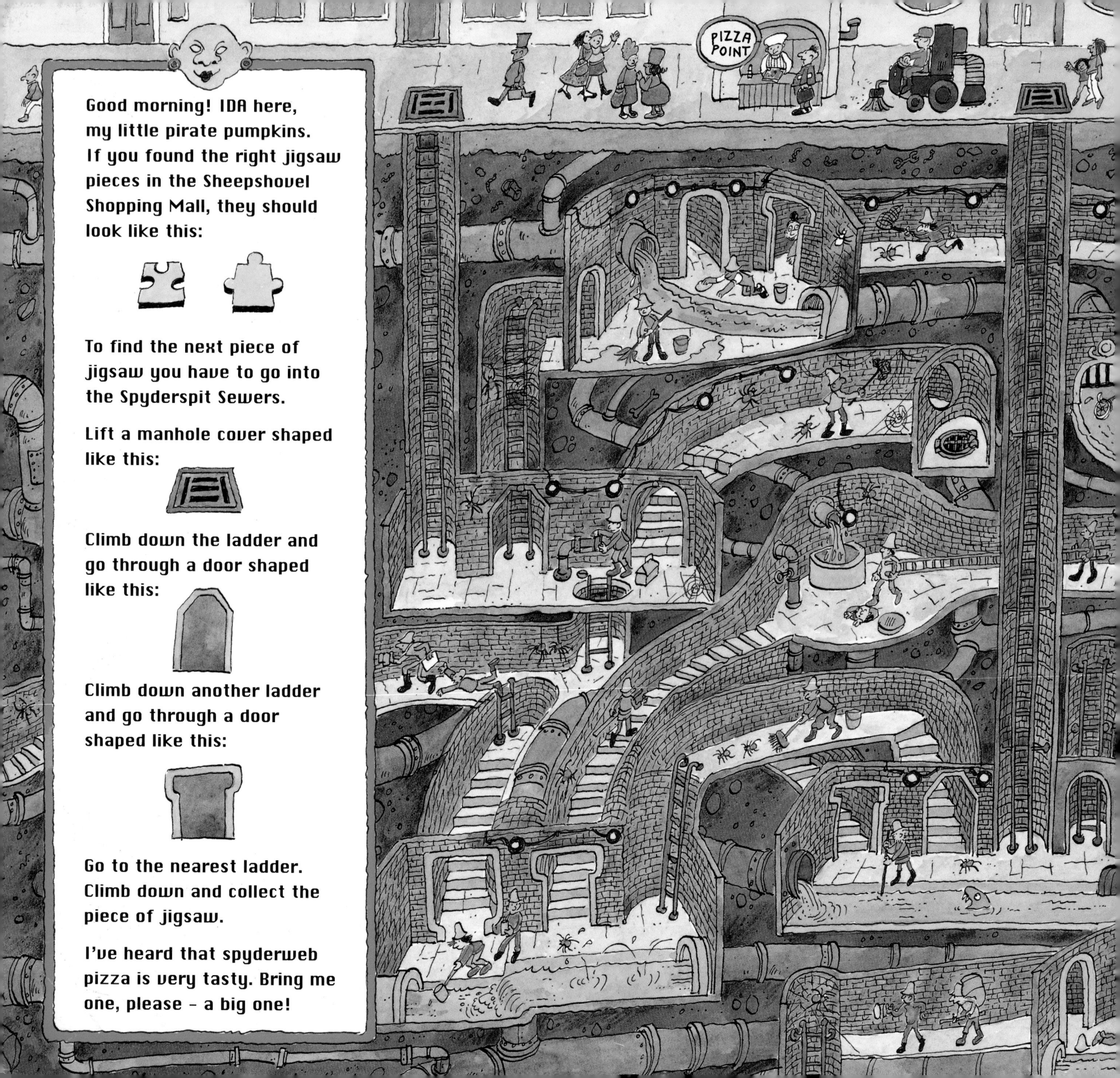

Good morning! IDA here, my little pirate pumpkins. If you found the right jigsaw pieces in the Sheepshovel Shopping Mall, they should look like this:

To find the next piece of jigsaw you have to go into the Spyderspit Sewers.

Lift a manhole cover shaped like this:

Climb down the ladder and go through a door shaped like this:

Climb down another ladder and go through a door shaped like this:

Go to the nearest ladder. Climb down and collect the piece of jigsaw.

I've heard that spyderweb pizza is very tasty. Bring me one, please – a big one!

PIZZA POINT

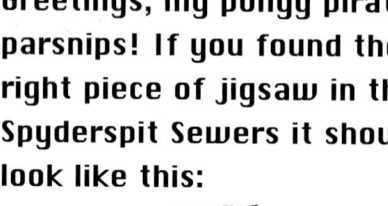

Greetings, my pongy pirate parsnips! If you found the right piece of jigsaw in the Spyderspit Sewers it should look like this:

Welcome to Badgerbat Bay. Watch out for the shoals of airfish!

Borrow an airfisherman's boat from a jetty shaped like this:

Use the compass below to find the right directions.

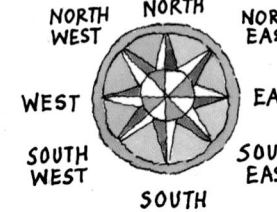
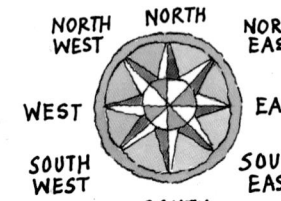

Sail north to a communications tower.

Sail north-east to a wind turbine.

Sail east to an airfish rock.

Sail south-west to a swimming pavilion and find the piece of jigsaw.

I know a lovely recipe for seaweed sausages!

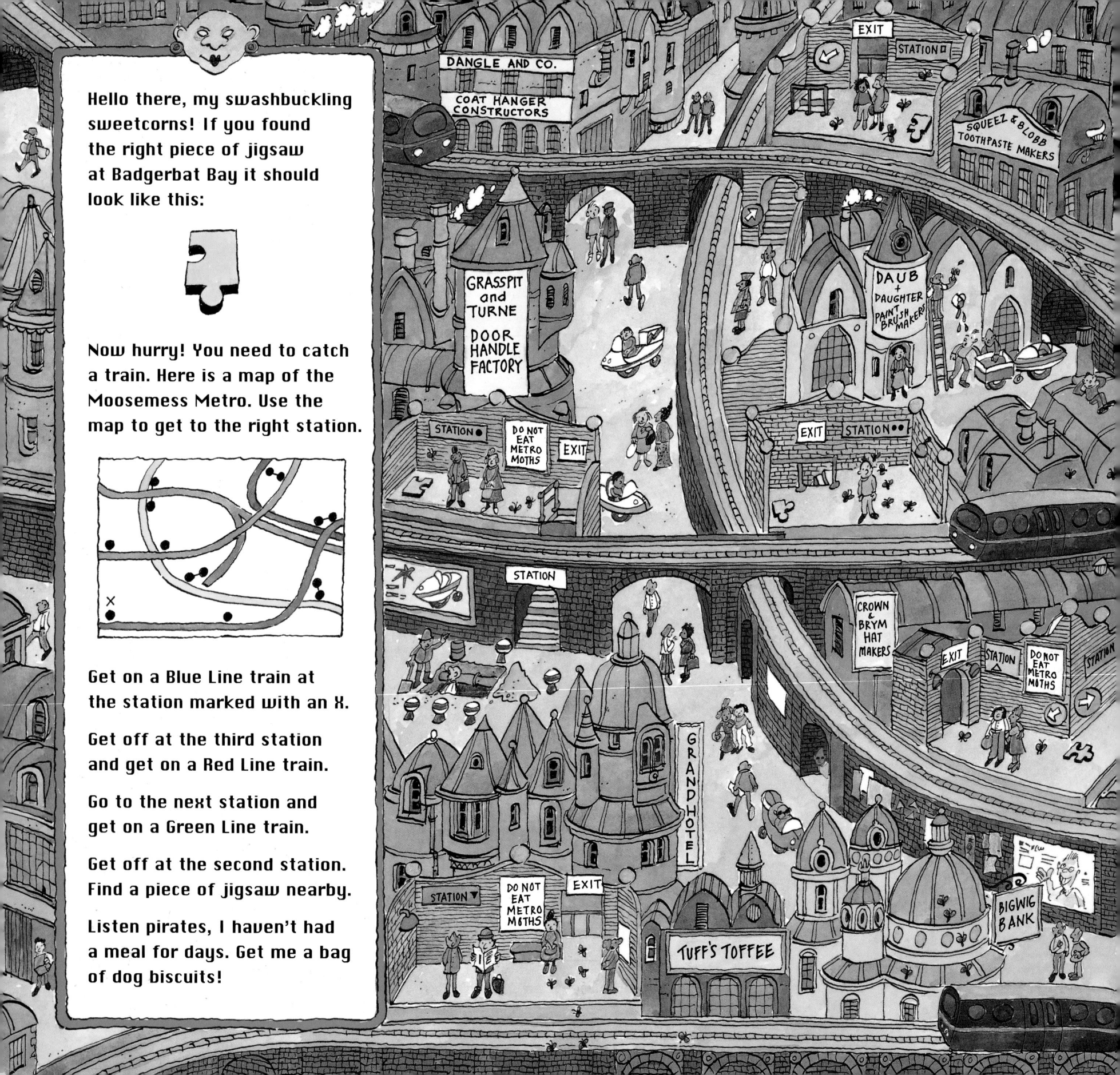

Hello there, my swashbuckling sweetcorns! If you found the right piece of jigsaw at Badgerbat Bay it should look like this:

Now hurry! You need to catch a train. Here is a map of the Moosemess Metro. Use the map to get to the right station.

Get on a Blue Line train at the station marked with an X.

Get off at the third station and get on a Red Line train.

Go to the next station and get on a Green Line train.

Get off at the second station. Find a piece of jigsaw nearby.

Listen pirates, I haven't had a meal for days. Get me a bag of dog biscuits!

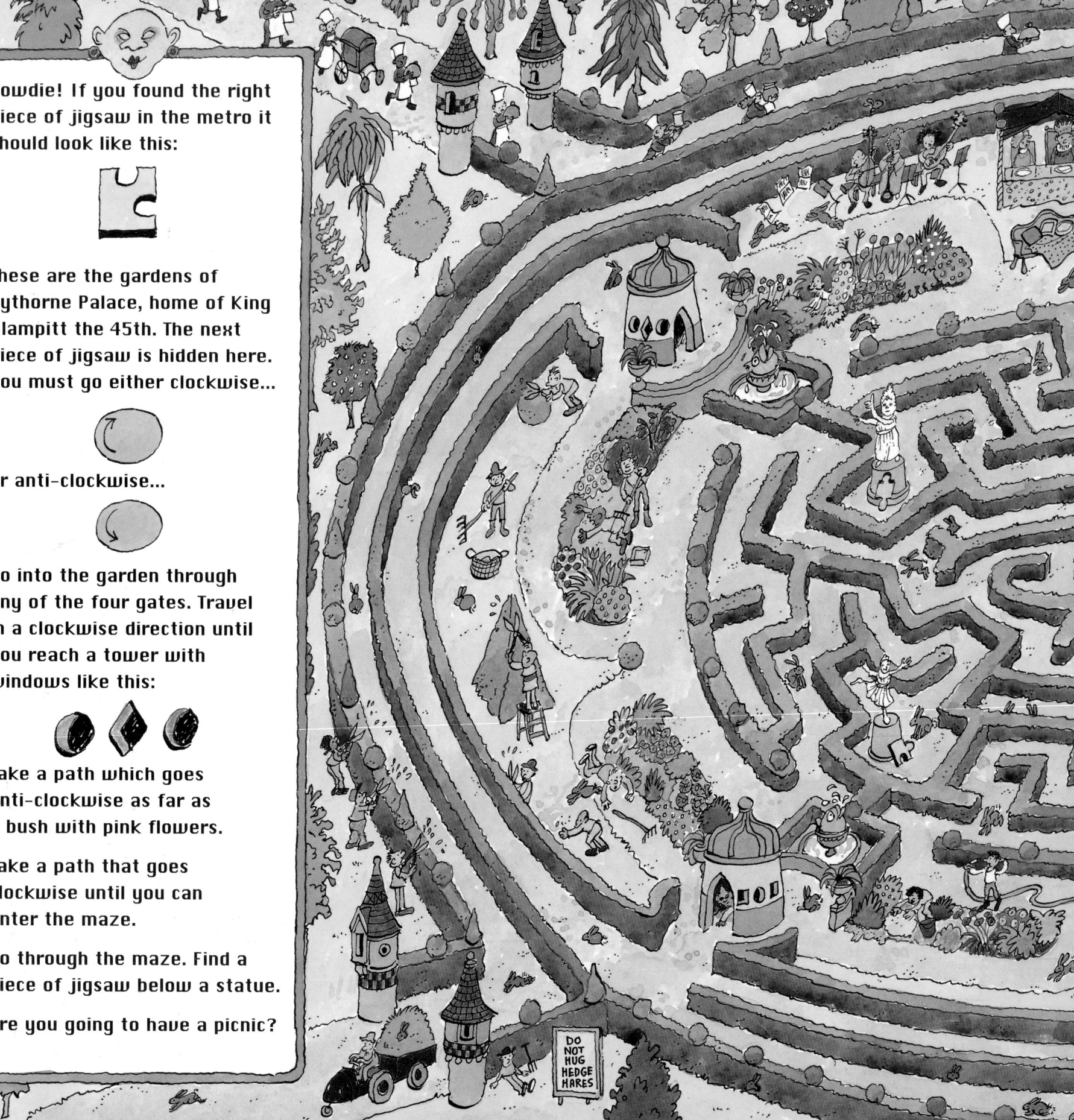

Howdie! If you found the right piece of jigsaw in the metro it should look like this:

These are the gardens of Pythorne Palace, home of King Klampitt the 45th. The next piece of jigsaw is hidden here. You must go either clockwise...

or anti-clockwise...

Go into the garden through any of the four gates. Travel in a clockwise direction until you reach a tower with windows like this:

Take a path which goes anti-clockwise as far as a bush with pink flowers.

Take a path that goes clockwise until you can enter the maze.

Go through the maze. Find a piece of jigsaw below a statue.

Are you going to have a picnic?

DO NOT HUG HEDGE HARES

Hello, my cheerful chipolatas! If you found the correct piece of jigsaw at the Pythorne Palace, it should look like this:

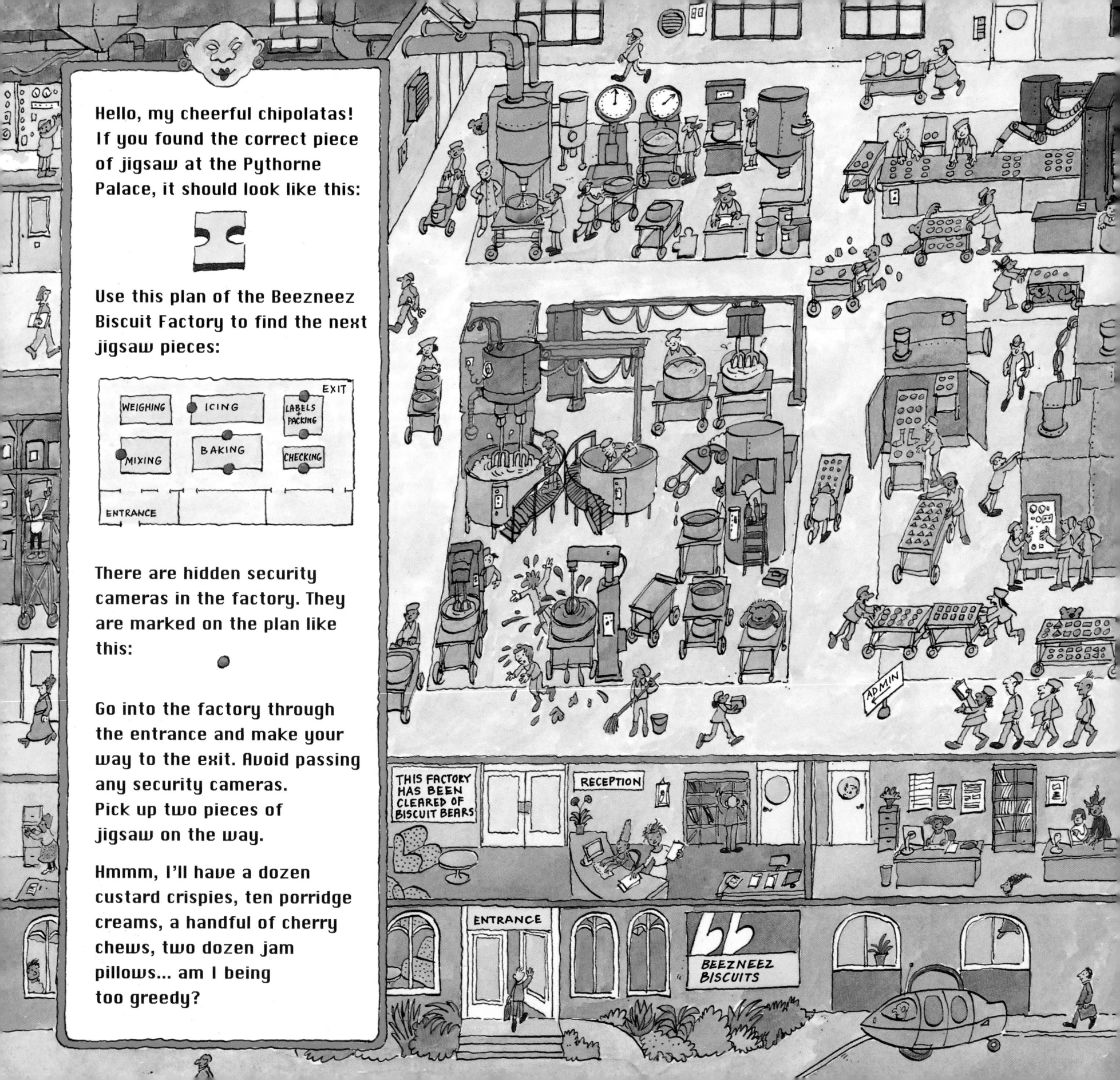

Use this plan of the Beezneez Biscuit Factory to find the next jigsaw pieces:

EXIT

WEIGHING   ICING   LABELS + PACKING

MIXING   BAKING   CHECKING

ENTRANCE

There are hidden security cameras in the factory. They are marked on the plan like this:

Go into the factory through the entrance and make your way to the exit. Avoid passing any security cameras.
Pick up two pieces of jigsaw on the way.

Hmmm, I'll have a dozen custard crispies, ten porridge creams, a handful of cherry chews, two dozen jam pillows... am I being too greedy?

THIS FACTORY HAS BEEN CLEARED OF BISCUIT BEARS

RECEPTION

ADMIN

ENTRANCE

BEEZNEEZ BISCUITS

Hello, my daring little pirate doughnuts! If you got the right pieces of jigsaw at the Beezneez Biscuit factory, they should look like this:

The next piece of jigsaw is on the slowball pitch. Use the map below to help you find it. The map has a grid on it. If I say go to D3, you must go along ➞ to box D and down ↓ to box 3.

A B C D E F G H
1
2 PENALTY PATH
3 DRIBBLING LANES   DRIBBLING LANES ➞
4
5
6

Join the dribbling lane at B1 and go to the end at D4.

Take the penalty path at D3 and go to E2.

Join another dribbling lane at F2 and go to H5. Pick up the piece of jigsaw nearby.

The teams are bound to have something tasty at half-time. Pass some along to me!

PITCH PIGEON CONTROL

BALL WAGON

Greetings, my clever piratical cabbages! If you found the right piece of jigsaw at the slowball pitch, it should look like this:

I think you deserve a night out in Skwidskwish Square - but take a measuring stick with you! You will need it to find the next piece of jigsaw. Here is the scale:

0 1 2 3 4 5 6
FOOTMOVES

Start from the little bit of chewing gum below a statue in the middle of the square. Go to a drainpipe 11 footmoves away.

Climb up the drainpipe for 9 footmoves.

Walk along the ledge for 16 footmoves.

Climb a statue and find a jigsaw piece.

There are lots of restaurants around here. Bring me back a handful of menus - they are very tasty!

Hello! IDA here, my fearless little fish fingers. If you found the right piece of jigsaw at Skwidskwish Square it should look like this:

Your quest is almost over. To find the last piece of jigsaw you must go to the Malswomp Caves where all sorts of nasty things lurk.

Go through the gateway.

Take the second path on the right and go to where the path forks.

At the fork, take the path as far as Skull Rock.

After Skull Rock, turn left at every fork until you find the piece of jigsaw.

It doesn't look as if there is anything tasty here. I hope you've brought a picnic — some Toadfil sandwiches would be nice.

BLUESTONE QUARRY CO.

BEWARE OF ROCKTOPUSES

WARNING! DRAGONERD ALERT! WHEN SIREN SOUNDS TAKE COVER

Puzzle

Space Pirates and the Treasure of Salmagundy
Scoular Anderson

Join Pirate Captain Tosca and her motley crew as they go in search of the clues to find the missing pirate treasure. Each challenge helps to teach basic mapping skills. Solve the puzzles and get the four friends to the treasure before evil pirate One Hand Hulke gets his hand and hook on the booty. Map reading has never been so much fun!

Fearless Dave
Bob Wilson

Princess Peach has a problem – a squeaky, cheese-eating problem – and requires a brave knight to rescue her. Dave's mum thinks that Dave is perfect for the job but he isn't so sure. Will Dave save the day and win the heart of the fair princess?

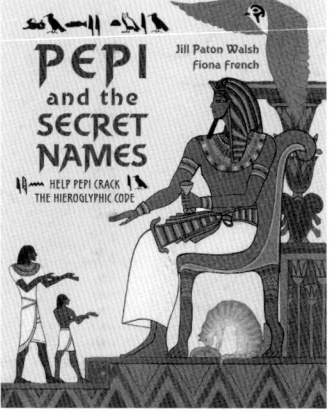

Pepi and the Secret Names
Jill Paton Walsh
Illustrated by Fiona French

Prince Dhutmose has commanded a splendid tomb to be built for his final journey to the Land of the Dead. Pepi's father is to decorate it, but how can he paint the unimaginable – the Lions of the Horizon, the terrible gods Horus the Hawk and Sebek the Crocodile, and Mertseger the deadly Winged Cobra? Pepi decides to find real-life models for his father, using his knowledge of secret names…

Frances Lincoln titles are available from all good bookshops. You can also buy books and find out more about your favourite titles, authors and illustrators on our website: www.franceslincoln.com